POSTER-A-PAGE™

Practice Makes Princess

Time
HOME ENTERTAINMENT

Publisher Jim Childs
Vice President, Brand & Digital Strategy Steven Sandonato
Executive Director, Marketing Services Carol Pittard
Executive Director, Retail & Special Sales Tom Mifsud
Executive Publishing Director Joy Bomba
Director, Bookazine Development & Marketing Laura Adam
Vice President, Finance Vandana Patel
Publishing Director Megan Pearlman
Assistant General Counsel Simone Procas
Assistant Director, Special Sales Ilene Schreider
Senior Brand Manager Nina Fleishman Reed
Senior Production Manager Susan Chodakiewicz
Associate Prepress Manager Alex Voznesenskiy

Editorial Director Stephen Koepp
Senior Editor Roe D'Angelo
Copy Chief Rina Bander
Design Manager Anne-Michelle Gallero
Editorial Operations Gina Scauzillo

SPECIAL THANKS
Katherine Barnet, Brad Beatson, Jeremy Biloon, Rose
Cirrincione, Assu Etsubneh, Christine Font, Susan Hettleman,
Hillary Hirsch, David Kahn, Jean Kennedy, Amy Mangus,
Kimberly Marshall, Nina Mistry, Dave Rozzelle, Ricardo
Santiago, Holly Smith, Adriana Tierno

PRODUCED BY
DOWNTOWN
BOOKWORKS INC.

President Julie Merberg
Publisher Patty Brown
Editorial Director Sarah Parvis
Assistant Editor Sara DiSalvo

DESIGNED BY Georgia Rucker Design

ISBN 10: 1-61893-375-2
ISBN 13: 978-1-61893-375-1

We welcome your comments and suggestions about Time Home
Entertainment Books. Please write to us at:
Time Home Entertainment Books
Attention: Book Editors
P.O. Box 11016
Des Moines, IA 50336-1016
If you would like to order any of our hardcover Collector's
Edition books, please call us at 800-327-6388, Monday through
Friday, 7 a.m.–8 p.m., or Saturday, 7 a.m.–6 p.m., Central Time.

1 QGS 14

Would you like to wear a magical amulet like Sofia does? Can you imagine spending the day with Clover? Or riding flying horses with Sofia and James? Flip through these pages and relive your favorite scenes with Sofia and her friends.

In a Poster-A-Page book, each page is perfect for decorating your room or playroom. Plus, there are nine supersize posters inside. Enjoy!

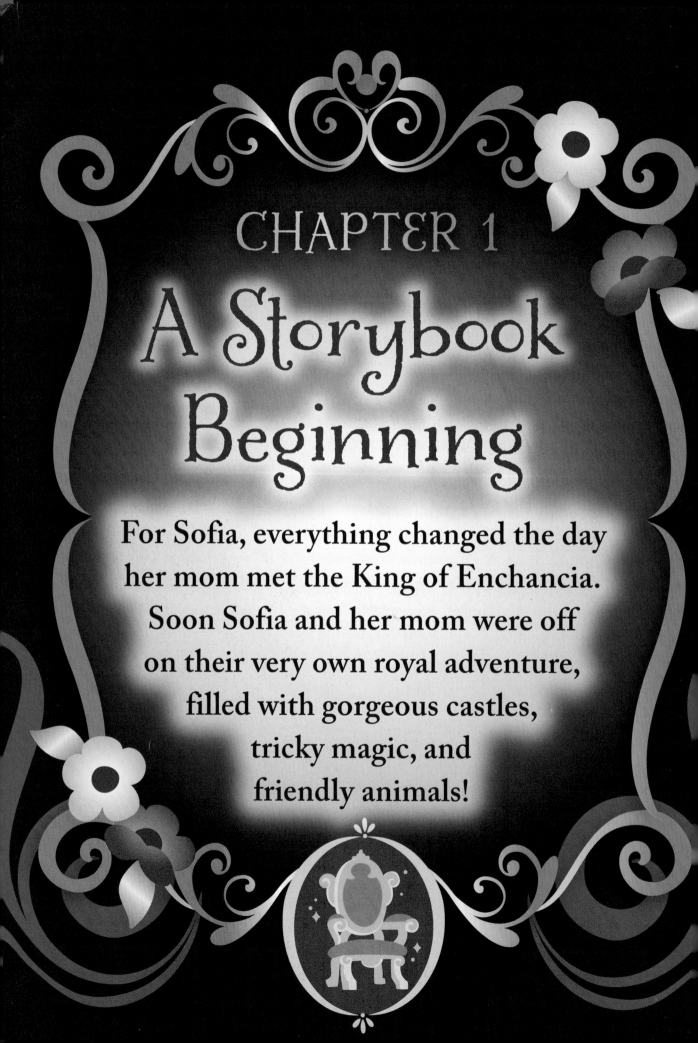

CHAPTER 1

A Storybook Beginning

For Sofia, everything changed the day her mom met the King of Enchancia. Soon Sofia and her mom were off on their very own royal adventure, filled with gorgeous castles, tricky magic, and friendly animals!

Welcome to Enchancia!

Meet Miranda.

Here's King Roland.

Welcome to the family, Sofia!

The Royal Life

All hail Queen Miranda and Princess Sofia!

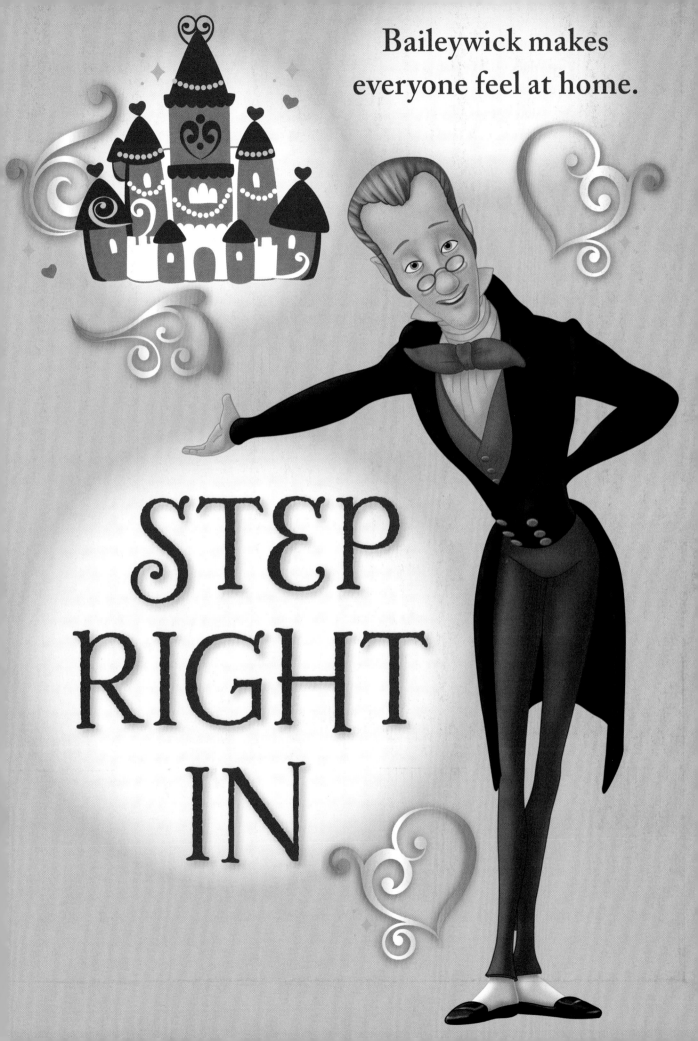

Baileywick makes
everyone feel at home.

STEP RIGHT IN

In the center of
the castle is a great big room.
At one end of the room, there are
five big, beautiful chairs.
One of them is just for me.

My very own throne!

Dresses
Galore

Introducing Amber

She's stylish and smart. She loves to wear pretty dresses and sparkling tiaras.

James is loyal and kind.
He likes to play games and have fun.
"Good morrow," says James.

Ruby and Jade

They are thoughtful and sweet.
Every day with them is a treat!

Friends Forever

Sisters are forever friends.

Friendship rules!

King Roland gave me the most special gift of all, a beautiful purple amulet. It sparkles and shines and gives me special powers. I can talk to animals! I'll wear it always.

Let the adventures begin!

Every day I spend with Clover is a wonderful day.
Thanks to the Amulet of Avalor, I speak bunny.

WHATNAUGHT

A very special squirrel

King Roland welcomed Sofia into his life.

May I have this dance?

Suddenly Royal

Cedric
A real, live sorcerer!

One day
I'll battle
dragons!

Life is
enchanting.

Life can change
in an instant.

I love my friends,
old and new.

Princesses are always
kind and true.

CHAPTER 2

Learning the Royal Way

There are so many new things to discover in the classrooms of Royal Prep and on the grounds of the castle. Luckily, Sofia is clever and loves to learn new things.

From riding flying horses to casting spells, there are so many wonderful things to learn.

Royal
Prep

Learning is enchanting.

Flora, Fauna, and Merryweather

are patient and kind.

They always keep their students in mind.

They solve any problems that might arise.

These magical teachers are
caring and wise.

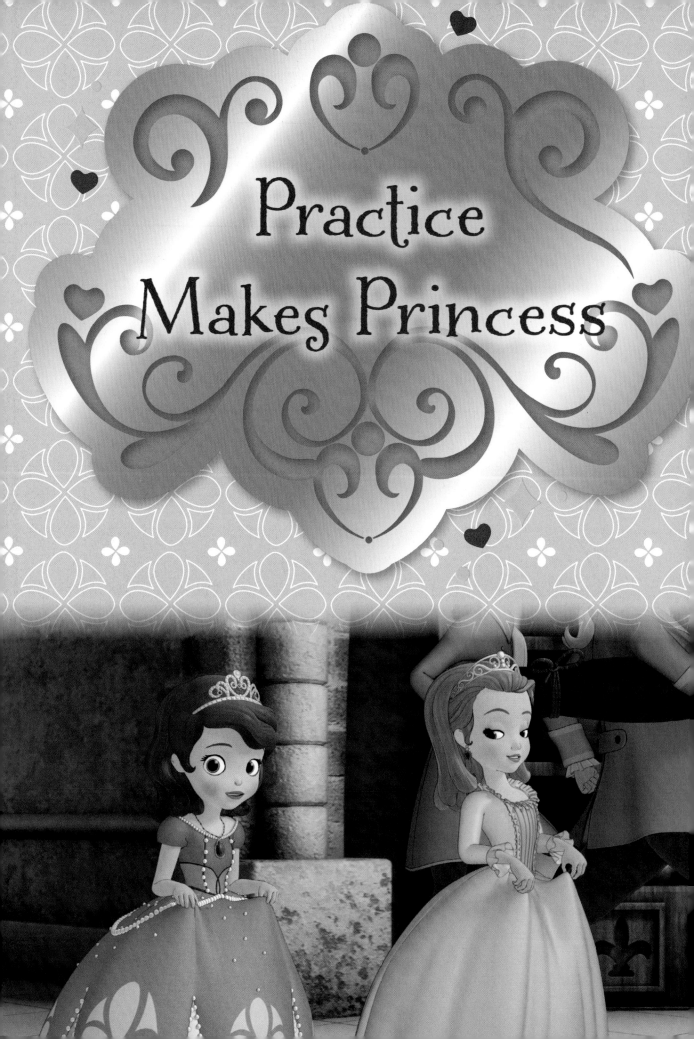

Practice Makes Princess

Follow
my lead.

Make
Magic

Take a Whirl on the Dance Floor

It's good to be looked after.

The world's full
of wonders waiting
to be seen.

Sometimes being a princess can be hard work.

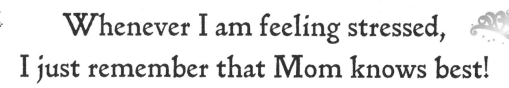

Whenever I am feeling stressed,
I just remember that Mom knows best!

I can always be myself
with my best buddies.

TEA TIME
with Sofia

Princess
in Training

Being royal comes from the heart.

Princesses
are honest and sweet.

Princesses
help others.

Princesses
are
gracious.

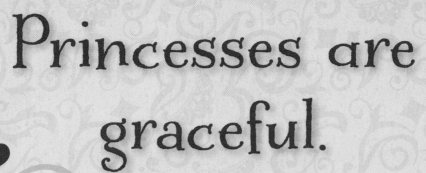

Princesses are graceful.

Princesses are
kind to animals.

Princesses love to learn.

A princess
always tries her best.

Ready to be a Princess

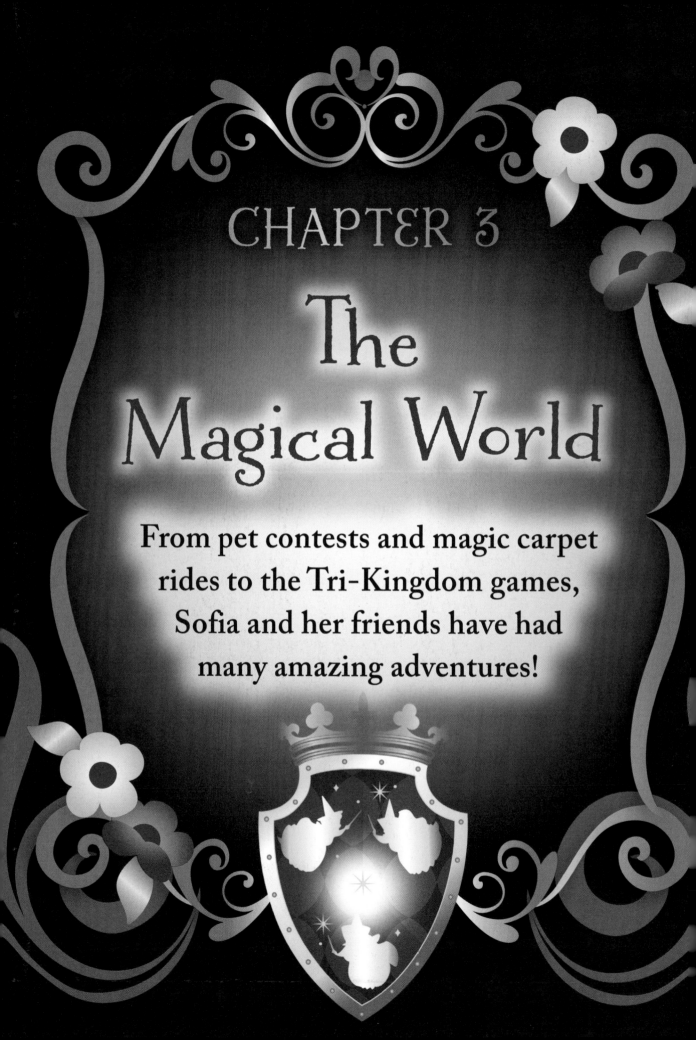

CHAPTER 3

The Magical World

From pet contests and magic carpet rides to the Tri-Kingdom games, Sofia and her friends have had many amazing adventures!

Minimus is a magical horse.
He is funny and sweet.

Practice hard, fly fast,
and always be royal!

I believe that anything
can be a princess thing.

Horses, on your wings, get set, GO!

A princess can do anything a prince does
if she keeps trying and never gives up.

Welcome
to the Castle!

FUN
is the name
of the game!

Stylish, But Regal

Let the
good times
troll!

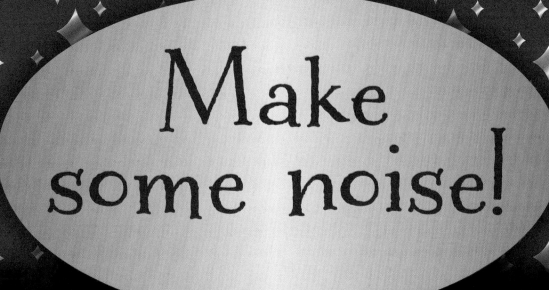

Make some noise!

Meet Teeni.

Sofia helps Teeni see stars for the very first time.

Princesses treat everyone like royalty.

Lend a helping hand.

What's more royal
than being brave?

Life is
magical.

It's Cedric, as in Cedric.

Wave your wand
with confidence.

I know just the
right spell.

I'm Crackle,
and I'm really excited
to meet you.

I'll have my princess call your princess.

I'm so glad we found a way

to make this the perfect day.

Making friends makes me happy!

THE TRI-KINGDOM GAMES

Let the games begin!

Flying Horseshoe Toss

Tri-Kingdom Volleyball

Teammates

And the winner is...

Best in Show

Strut, strut, strut,
and pose!

SHIMMER!

I can always
count on YOU!

There's a lot of toughness crammed into this soft, fluffy package.

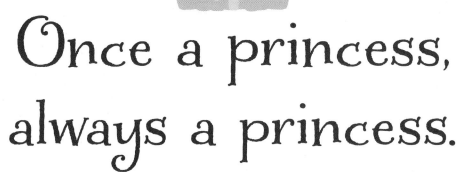

Once a princess, always a princess.

Let your imagination
SOAR!

I wish
it was your
birthday
every day.

I'm not good
at apologies.
Pranks, I can do.

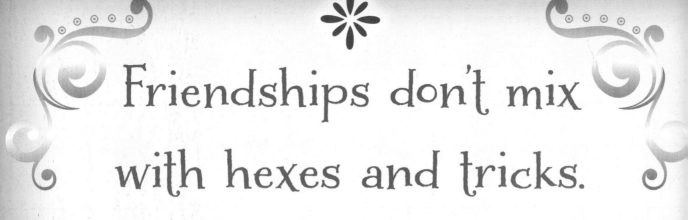

Friendships don't mix with hexes and tricks.

Friends always
help each other.

I can't wait to dance
at the ball tonight.

It's the castle jewel room.
My favorite room in
the whole kingdom!

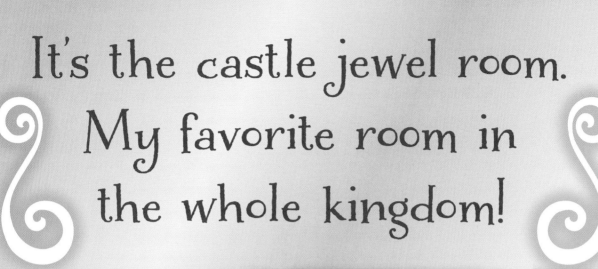

How will I
ever choose?

I love
sparkly
things.

We've got paws!
And we've got claws!
Let's help Sofia!

I'm a princess.
I can do anything!

COSTUME CONTEST!

Princess
Butterfly

CHAPTER 4

Decorate Your Castle

Posters featuring Sofia, Amber, Clover, and the whole gang from Enchancia can brighten up any room. Pick your favorites, hang them up, and make your space shine!

Welcome to the palace.

Make yourself at home.

Melodies are made here.

Rise and Shine

The early bird gets the worm.

Enchanted by everything!

Opportunity hops.

Behind this door,
there lies
magic!

ENTER AT YOUR OWN RISK!

I'm practicing spells.

Don't forget our motto:
Rule over others as you'd
have them rule over you.

Every task, every test—
just give it your best.

Kindness practiced
HERE

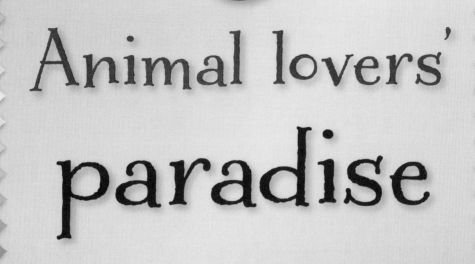

Animal lovers' paradise

The Belle of the Ball

True friends are a treasure.

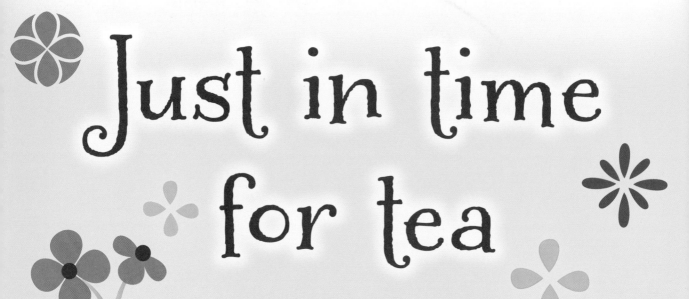

Just in time for tea

Let's celebrate!

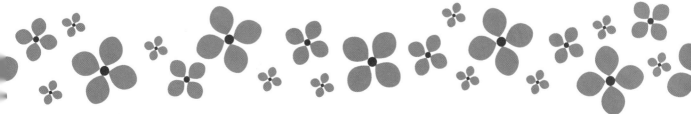

A princess can do anything
she sets her mind to.

I just love getting dressed up!

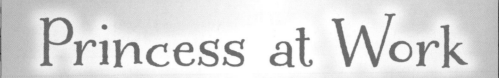

Princess at Work

Homework Zone

I'll be down in a minute.
I am working on my masterpiece.

See you soon!